The Knight of the Wild

Her First Knight, Volume 1

Ash Gray

Published by Ash Gray, 2022.

THE KNIGHT OF THE WILD

First edition. September 14, 2022.

Copyright © 2022 Ash Gray.

ISBN: 979-8224996018

Written by Ash Gray.

Chapter 1

Princess Ava stood outside the war chamber in her father's castle, listening with her head slightly tilted as the men on the other side of the enormous wooden doors argued back and forth about the best course of action to take should the armies of Realm Endoreth finally reach the capital. Endoreth's armies had been marching on Realm Illa for an entire year, and after only one year, were on the brink of taking the realm. For Ava's father, it was a supreme embarrassment.

Most of Realm Illa had lost faith in King Eyvor's ability to defend them and had fled to Realm Endoreth or into the wild country altogether, so terrified were they of the ever-encroaching armies of King Bjorn. The southern king's armies were ruthless and evil, killing peasants and raping women, killing children and raiding shops, burning farms along the countryside. They were no better than raiders and bandits, it was said. Things were so bad, in fact, that Princess Ava's father had been planning to marry her off quickly to Prince Cassian of Realm Almara to secure an alliance and thus end the invasion.

And so, Princess Ava stood in the torchlit corridor with her handmaiden, Lysa, listening anxiously to the deep voices in the war room and praying to the gods above that her father didn't still intend to marry her off. She was the most desired princess in the seven kingdoms, with long blonde hair that fell to her backside, tiny hands and feet, a sweet, heart-shaped face, and great breasts practically pouring from the laces of her pink gown. Even now, the female guards who stood nearby, pretending not to notice her, were straining to keep themselves dry in their smallclothes.

But Princess Ava didn't notice how the guards struggled, though, nor did she notice how often Lysa glanced at her with soft-eyed appreciation. Lysa was a small, mousey little woman, quite young, with short brown hair and soft brown eyes, often nervous and strained by the antics of her princess. Even now, she wrung her hands on her apron and hissed miserably, "My princess! We mustn't! We'll be caught for sure—!"

"Then hush and keep watch!" Princess Ava snapped impatiently without looking away from the door, and Lysa hushed and bit her lip, turning a little pink.

At last, Princess Ava's green eyes grew round when she heard her father mention her.

"—precisely why I have summoned a personal bodyguard for my daughter," the king was saying gruffly. "If the capital is taken, *Ava* will be taken! And I shall die before my daughter is ravished by that foul *heathen* who calls himself a king! The stories they tell of that *brute*—"

"But, your majesty," said a man, and Ava recognized the soft, agreeable voice of her father's chamberlain, "it's too late to smuggle her from the city now! King Bjorn's men are so close, they're practically at the gate—!"

"No!" the king snapped, and the table thumped, as if he had slammed his gauntlet on it. "I shall *not* let that brute have her, do you hear me? King Elric has agreed to marry Cassian to my Ava—"

Ava gasped miserably. Beside her, Lysa put a comforting hand on her shoulder.

"—and is already sending knights to aid us! Elric is as desperate for this alliance as we are, make no mistake," went on the king confidently. "Who do you think Bjorn will turn on next when he's done burning my realm? And if Ava were to perish, there would be no chance of an alliance. She is my only daughter . . ." The king paused sadly, and Ava looked at the little slippers that peeped from under her skirts: her mother had died giving birth to her, a wound which had never healed in the king.

"Your majesty, you could always remarry," said the chamberlain gently. "You are still quite young, and there are many eager and willing—"

"Silence, Godwin, for the sake of the gods!" the king snapped. "I have summoned my daughter's new bodyguard. The woman shall have already arrived, I think—"

"I beg pardon, but a *woman*, your majesty?" pipped up the chamberlain. He sounded very confused, even appalled.

"Yes!" snapped the king. "Do you think I'd trust a man alone with my daughter day and night? A man standing over her as she did sleep?"

"No knight with any honor would *dare* touch the princess of Illa!" cried another voice in amazement. This time, it was Captain Kenric, the captain of the royal guard. "One of my men would never—! They are sworn to protect—!" he blustered on, outraged.

"Be that as it may, Kenric," said the king, sternly but soothingly, "imagine what would happen if my daughter fell in love with her bodyguard and then did get it in her fool-head to bed him? It has happened before with queens and their guards. Or have you forgotten my mother?"

There was silence in the room, and Princess Ava swallowed hard. She had heard the story a thousand times: her grandmother, the late Queen Avaria, had been caught in the act of bedding her bodyguard. Her husband, King Theodoric, had her beheaded alongside her bodyguard in the capital square in order to save face (rumor had it he hadn't even cared much and perhaps had known all along).

Queen Avaria's affair wasn't the first time such a thing had happened in House Damaris. The women of the family were notorious for their sexual rebellion. Many romanticized and admired them for it, but only once they had been punished and were dead and gone—No one wanted to appear as if they truly approved of the behavior.

"They call her the Knight of the Wild," went on the king, who sounded as proud as if he were the knight's father. "For her country and her family's sigil, the wild hart. House Rossi is from Realm Wildoras! Isn't that fascinating?"

"I hope this woman is an exceptional warrior," grumbled Captain Kenric, who still sounded a little bitter that his own knights weren't to be trusted.

The king seemed to pick up on Kenric's bitterness and said in amusement, "That she is, Kenric. Graduated from the academy the top in her class—" The king halted when there was a spraying, raspberry sound: someone had spit out their wine.

"The t-top?" sputtered Chamberlain Godwin. "The *top* in her glass? Out of hundreds? You mean to tell me she did outmatch the men?"

The king chuckled. "I told you she was exceptional. And I would have it no other way. Only the best for my daughter!"

Captain Kenric snorted. "What? Is she some sort of giant, then? A manly beast of a woman, I suppose?"

Princess Ava cringed at the very thought and quickly turned away, hurrying back down the corridor and toward her bedchamber. Lysa hurried to keep pace with her, carrying her long pink train as they nearly raced down the stairs. When they were a safe distance from the war chamber, Lysa said breathlessly, "Your highness, I don't understand why this upsets you!"

Princess Ava kept walking very quickly, the better to reach her bedchamber before her father learned she had left it. Hearing Lysa's words, she realized with a flush of shame that her cheeks were indeed wet with tears. She angrily wiped the tears away with her kerchief, but her pale lashes kept blinking them out, so that her green eyes shimmered.

"Why shouldn't I be upset, Lysa? My father is marrying me off like chattel—!" Ava paused when she reached the double doors of her bedchamber at last. The two guards standing there muttered, "Your highness . . ." as they pulled the doors open for her. Princess Ava swept in at the same rapid pace, and Lysa staggered to keep up, still bearing her train.

"—and now I shall have some overbearing babysitter constantly underfoot!" Princess Ava went on bitterly and threw her kerchief almost violently to the floor.

"But at least it shall be a woman," soothed Lysa, scrambling after her. "I know you don't fancy men, and having one around all the time would be horrid—"

"Ha! As if this woman were any better! Knights are all the same! And this one's a barbarian! She is likely some big hairy oaf with a hog's face who shall constantly follow me round, telling me what to do, and—!" The words halted in Ava's mouth.

A red-haired woman in silver armor was standing beside the great arched windows in the stone wall, her hands behind her back, calmly observing Princess Ava and Lysa. . . and she was utterly beautiful.

"Your highness," said the woman. "I am the Knight of the Wild. I am your knight."

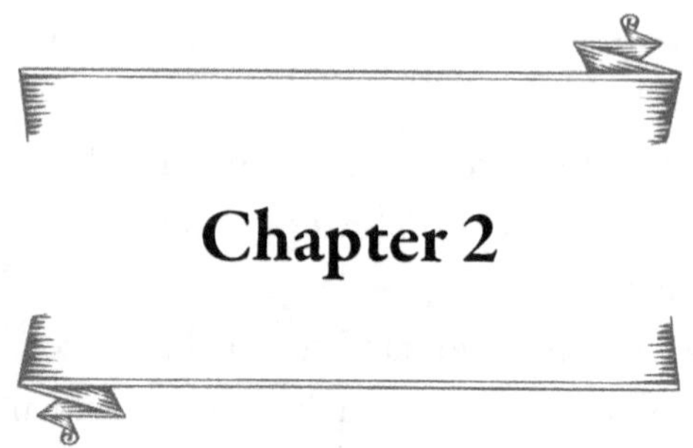

Chapter 2

The Knight of the Wild was tall and muscular and fit, standing there in full armor, at least six feet in height, a barbarian with warpaint swirling her cheek and her eye, and yet, her bone structure was delicate and feminine still. Pale morning light slanted over her piercing blue eyes and her red hair, which was half-plaited and pulled back in a thick, messy tail. A sword was on her hip, and resting against the wall at her foot was a shield with the bucking hart sigil of her house upon it.

"Your highness," the knight repeated in a deep alto that was soothing to Princess Ava's ears almost immediately. Ava felt a thump when the knight's intense eyes connected with her own. The woman's gaze completely paralyzed her, though she flushed a little with rage to see the laughter in the knight's eyes.

"You mock me, knight? Noble blood or no, I could have your head!" Ava warned.

The knight cast her eyes down. "No, your highness. I only marvel at your beauty. Your eyes did make the world cease for one tremulous moment."

Princess Ava flushed again, this time with pleasure, though she hated herself for it.

Smiling at Ava's embarrassment, the Knight of the Wild knelt dutifully on one knee, head down. "I await your blessing, fair princess," she said to the wooden floorboards. "If you find me too hairy or oafish, I shall humbly return to the academy and announce my shame."

Ava held back a laugh. "Oh, do get up," she said, rolling her eyes.

The knight rose to her feet again, placing her hands once more behind her back. Princess Ava looked at her, so dignified and composed, and thought she was awfully well-spoken for a barbarian from Wildoras. The people of Wildoras stubbornly kept to their own language, which often resulted in their common tongue being broken and lazy. It was also strange that the people of Wildoras should have sent one of their own to become a knight in Illa. Princess Ava looked at the woman, who couldn't have been more than twenty, and felt her curiosity aroused.

"What shall you have of me?" the knight politely asked.

Princess Ava realized with a start that the woman had been calmly studying her, watching her with those intense blue eyes, and her eyes were playful again . . . and warm with lust.

Princess Ava quivered behind her laces. She was a virgin. She had never been touched by a woman, she had never been kissed, though she had often dreamed of it. How many years had she spent, a teenage girl, watching the women knights in the training yard as their muscles flexed? Fierce eyes and hard bodies, all of them, and young Ava had wanted them, wanted their hard hands on her desperately. Now she was twenty-two – still untouched, still unwed due to her father's overprotective doting, and still . . . burning with desire. She looked at the Knight of the Wild and suspected she had bedded many a woman. It was the way in Wildoras. And the way the woman's hungry blue eyes devoured Ava's cleavage . . .

Holding down another humiliating blush, Princess Ava glided with as much dignity as she could to the fireplace, where she sat gracefully in a chair and gestured for Lysa to build up the fire. Lysa set down the princess' train and scrambled to obey, her mousey brown hair a tousled mess from their earlier rush down the stairs.

Ava realized with horror that she must've been a mess as well: she was likely mussed and tearstained. Feeling self-conscious, she quickly smoothed down her hair and her gown and was glad when the knight pretended not to notice, instead politely smiling and looking out the window.

"Do sit with me," Ava regally commanded and gestured at the chair opposite her own.

The knight obeyed, crossing the room with jingling armor and sitting opposite Ava. A second later, and a fire was roaring on the hearth. Lysa, breathless from her efforts, then sat on a low stool near Ava's chair and took up her knitting. She pretended to be occupied with it, but Ava noticed how she kept passing the knight admiring looks, and Ava couldn't blame the handmaiden: sitting there so tall and strong in her armor, the knight was a wonder to behold. She looked like some sort of legendary warrior out of a child's story, Ava thought. She was just too beautiful and wild and powerful to be real.

The knight was sitting mannishly with her knees wide apart, wild red hair spilling over one shoulder like fire. Her blue eyes were staring almost intently at Ava's face again. It made Ava's sex throb, and she held down a blush of arousal.

"I-I suppose if you are to be my knight that I should know your name," said Princess Ava, trying to keep her composure and feeling like a fool.

"I am Liadan Rossi, your highness," answered the knight politely.

"Yes, the Rossies," said Ava thoughtfully. "So mild-mannered for a barbarian, aren't you?" she observed in amusement.

Liadan smiled, her blue eyes firing prettily. "If you would have me behave otherwise, your highness . . ."

Ava blushed hotly.

The knight chuckled in her deep alto. "Forgive me, your highness. We barbarians have no shame," she said and paused, piercing Ava with her hungry gaze again.

Ava's heart fluttered and she fanned her long, pale lashes down. Was this what it was like for the other maidens at the balls? Who flirted and teased the men? She had always watched in envy, wishing to know what it was like to exchange such dirty banter, to be desired by someone she could desire back. Often times, she would find herself enduring the attention of some thirsty prince whose advances she found appalling, whose flirting she found annoying or simply exhausting. The princes never took "no" for an answer, and many assumed she was playing hard-to-get, when in reality, she simply wasn't attracted to men.

Now, for first time in her life, someone was flirting with Ava, making her feel wanted, and rather than being annoying or repulsive, it was the most wonderful, intense thing in the world. The Knight of the Wild kept looking at her as if she wanted to devour her, as if she had never quite seen a woman like Ava before.

Shivering a little under the knight's gaze, Ava hesitated, glanced down at her skirts, and feeling like a silly girl, she fumbled with them as she said, "And if I were to command you to behave otherwise . . .?"

The knight did not look away. "Then I would get on my knees and obey. Most readily, your highness."

Ava bit her lip against a giggle and felt the heat creeping up her face. The knight was gazing at her so intensely, she shyly lowered her pale lashes, but she could still feel the woman's gaze, how strongly she wanted Ava, as if a hot light were upon her, and she tried to control her breath. Her cleavage was heaving a little.

The knight wanted Ava and had just made it clear that she would lay with her if beckoned. Was this it? Would Ava finally . . . know a lover's touch? Ava's heart was pounding in her chest so hard it hurt.

"But I am the princess of Realm Illa," Ava said, finding the courage to lift her face, letting her shyness fall away. "If you and I were found together, my father would behead you! Does that not frighten you?"

Liadan only smiled. "I think it would be a worthy death, your highness, to taste the softness of your lips."

Ava's heart leapt as she realized which lips the knight meant. She bit her lip and looked down again, trying not to smile, ignoring how Lysa watched them both with her mouth hanging open, the silly fool.

Ava frowned and pushed her feelings of desire down. "No, no . . ." she said, suddenly rising. What was she thinking? She couldn't lay with this knight, no matter how beautiful and breathtaking she was! She was the princess of Illa! Hate it as she did, she must remain untouched for her wedding night, she must honor her husband and her duty as future queen of Almara! For if they began a tryst and were discovered, there would be no mercy!

Ava turned her back to the knight and faced the fire. The heat was soothing as it spread over her face and neck, down her front, over her hands, which she fiddled with miserably. "We should not continue such talk, even in jest," she said unhappily. "I am to wed Prince Cassian. We shall rule Almara together and have many fine children."

The Knight of the Wild was silent. There was a faint jingle of armor, nothing more.

"If you are to be my bodyguard, we must build a bond that is one of formality and friendship, nothing more," Ava went on with a shaking breath. She glanced to the arched windows where the knight had been standing only minutes before. The sun was rising high in the sky. "Lysa," she said, "my noon meal should be ready. Run down to the kitchens and see."

"Yes, your highness!" Lysa shrilled and bounced up, leaving the room and closing the great doors behind her. She gave Ava and the knight a little smirk before closing the doors – a smirk which annoyed Ava to no end.

Lysa seemed to think something was going to happen between Ava and the knight, but nothing could be farthest from the truth! She was not her grandmother! She had more discipline and . . . Ava went still when she heard the jingle of armor behind her. The knight had risen to her feet.

Ava swallowed hard and gazed at the fire. She was shaking a little. She could hear the knight's boots coming to her. "As I was saying," Ava went on regally and lifted her chin, "w-we must maintain a bond of formality and . . ."

Ava looked down: the knight's hands – now bare of their gauntlets – took the front of her gown in fistfuls and suddenly ripped it open, snapping the laces. Ava screamed softly as her great breasts shivered free, standing high, the little nipples hard from desire. The knight's pretty eyes narrowed, and she groped Ava's heavy breasts in hard fistfuls, kissing hotly, quickly on her neck. Ava's lashes fluttered in shock from the sudden flush of pleasure and she shivered, caught in the big woman's relentless grasp.

"The—the audacity!" Ava gasped, though clearly enjoying what was happening.

"By the gods, you have fine tits," the knight grunted between frantic kisses.

Ava squirmed against the pleasure as her breasts were groped hard. Her clitoris was pumping wildly now. She couldn't move, couldn't breathe. It felt . . . *exquisite* to be touched. She had expected such a strong woman to be rough but hadn't realized how much she would enjoy Liadan's strong fingers. She blushed to hear herself suddenly moan.

As she continued groping and massaging Ava's breast, the knight's other hand tore roughly at Ava's gown and slip, until they were a mound of pink and white fabric around Ava's ankles. Ava was now standing there in nothing but her linen panties, her sex throbbing and swollen with the blood of arousal, soft moans escaping her pink lips as she frowned against the pleasure. Both the knight's hands returned to massaging her breasts in fistfuls. Then without warning, one of Liadan's hands released her, leaving her breast to jiggle as it stood high. The hand slid down her trembling belly.

The princess watched, heart pounding faster and faster, as the knight's hand smoothed toward her panties and slid inside. She closed her eyes and gasped with delight when the knight's fingers slid into her sex and curled, fingering her so hard, her hips jerked from the motion.

She had never been touched before, and the pleasure paralyzed her. Her green eyes grew round and she stared into space, in shock as she was aggressively fingered and groped, as her neck was kissed. Her pumping clitoris was massaged by Liadan's careful fingers, then the fingers crammed in the heat and moisture of her sex yet again, roughly coaxing her to fuller arousal, and her head fell back with a cry of shocked delight.

Her clitoris was throbbing harder and faster from the knight's skilled fingers. Liadan's touch on her clitoris was hungry and yet gentle, insistent and yet soft, coaxing Ava to more intense arousal with each stroke. Eyes closed, Ava's pink lips opened wide and she gasped as she was pleasured, sex and nipple caressed and massaged. She trembled against it and could feel the hot moisture sliding down her thighs.

"Look at me," the knight whispered huskily.

Feeling suddenly very shy, Princess Ava opened her eyes only a little. Very slowly, she turned her head and looked into Liadan's face, and her heart skipped a beat: Liadan's blue eyes were blazing with lust. She kissed Ava roughly on the mouth, her tongue caressing hers so hard that Ava gulped on it and managed with a moan of pleasure to thrust her tongue in return. They were moaning through the passionate kiss when it happened: Liadan's strong fingers crammed hard through the moisture of Ava's sex, plunging with hunger so deep inside that Ava felt her sex clench on the woman's fingers and release.

Ava pulled her lips free to gasp. They looked in each other's eyes as Liadan fingered Ava to a panting climax, and her knight's blue eyes as they coaxed her to arousal were soft with a startling amount of affection.

Chapter 3

When Liadan awoke that morning, she was in Princess Ava's great four-poster bed, in nothing but her smallclothes: a linen bra and the bottom half of her woolen hose. Her red hair was a tousled mess, having been pulled loose of its tail by the eager princess, who thought it was so pretty, and her bare muscular arms and shoulders flexed as she sat up on her elbow and yawned.

Birds were singing beyond the flower-webbed windows, sunlight was streaming in fingers across the bed, and looking over, Liadan's eyes softened to see Ava lying there, naked and soft and beautiful beneath the dark pink coverlet, her blonde hair a golden mess across one eye. She was lying on her side, her great breasts swelling against each other under one slender arm, her expression peaceful. She looked like a beauty from a bard song. And she was perfect, Liadan thought, so shy and sweet and tender – while pretending to be so commanding and regal. The sound of her giggle always made Liadan's heart soar. Liadan had bedded maidens before in her years at the academy, while larking with her friends in taverns and at festivals, and while she had loved those women, she had never felt this way before and . . . Ava was going to wed a prince.

Many times had flustered and blushing young women given Liadan their favors, begged sweetly that she should be their knight, and so many times, Liadan had refused. Now the one woman Liadan wanted in all the world was the one woman she could not have. Such cruel irony. Perhaps the gods did despise the women of Wildoras after all.

It was said the Wildorans had been banished eons ago to live in the wild as punishment for attempting to rule the world with their magick power. No matter how they tried, they could not raise buildings and cities, for the structures always fell to ruin due to natural disaster, and the people of Wildoras were forced instead to live in camps, in the very trees and brush and grassland, and remain barbarians who cast spells.

Liadan sat up, looked wretchedly away from the sleeping princess, and rested her elbows on her knees as she looked around for the rest of her underarmor. She knew she should rise and dress. It would look suspicious if the princess stayed abed the day through . . . while locked away in the bedchamber with her bodyguard.

"Mmm," Princess Ava moaned. Liadan felt the princess' small hand rub her back. "Stay abed a while," the princess softly pleaded. "I am not due to see my father for another hour in the least. He will not suspect."

Liadan wanted to protest, but she liked the idea of stealing one more hour alone with the princess, if she could. She hesitated and laid back on the pillows. She smiled when Princess Ava reached over and took her hand.

"Now I know why you are the Knight of the Wild," Princess Ava said, gazing at Liadan with girlish delight from behind the sweep of her blonde hair.

Liadan chuckled softly, her deep alto rising against the crackle of the fire. "Wild was I, my princess?"

Ava blushed a little: she liked it when Liadan called her "my princess."

"They tell stories of the wild barbarians in Wildoras," said Ava. "I've heard them all. Father is fascinated with your people and is always going on about them. I suspect it's why he chose you. The Wildorans have very ancient blood, and the other realms used to live in fear of your people." Ava frowned. "But so few Wildorans come to Illa, my knight. Why leave your homeland?"

Liadan hesitated. She hadn't seen her homeland since she was six years old, and she was nearing her twenty-first birthday. How she missed it, the giant trees in the deep green forests . . . It was difficult to speak of it, the day she was forced to leave. She never even spoke of her exile to her friends at the knight academy. Even Ethne, her best friend, didn't know the entire story.

"I was exiled," Liadan said hoarsely.

Princess Ava was silent a moment: she hadn't expected that. "But knights begin training when they are little children. What could a child have done to deserve exile?"

"I was born," Liadan answered somberly. "You know I am of noble blood. In Wildoras, it is the women who lead the tribes, for there are no men, not like here. My mother the queen had many daughters. She did not want us fighting to become queen, so my eldest sister was allowed to stay and the rest of us were sent into the other realms to live our lives."

"So you have other sisters out there somewhere, sisters you haven't seen in years," said Princess Ava sympathetically.

"Aye. My favorite is serving as a knight in the temple in Hastow. Ceana. We use to write each other, but we sort of . . . drifted apart over the years."

Princess Ava's small hand squeezed Liadan's to comfort her, and the knight's lips curled in a small smile. The princess was such a sweet, compassionate thing. That she pretended to be so cold and regal was endlessly amusing to Liadan.

Liadan stared at the ceiling as she asked, "What sort of stories do they tell?" She had a feeling she would regret asking, however.

Ava hesitated, as if she regretted bringing up. "That you . . . sacrifice your children to the gods in exchange for magick power and . . . and it's why you're cursed to live as savages and . . ."

Liadan laughed more loudly than she intended to. "Is that what they say? Then your father is *mad* for choosing me from the academy."

"I don't think he believes the bad stories," Ava protested, "just the good stories! The Wildorans are said to be wild, fierce, and strong, the best warriors in the seven realms! The women have the strength of ten men!"

"Aye, that much is true," said Liadan, nodding. She reached over, and taking Ava by her tiny waist, she lifted her up in the air.

Ava fumbled to clutch Liadan's arms, and her eyes went round in shock, her cheeks flushed prettily at the ease with which she was lifted in the air like a doll. Her big breasts hung down, trembling against each other, and the pink nipples hardened. She seemed embarrassed by her own arousal and blushed even brighter as her golden hair draped down around her small, round face.

Liadan smiled and slowly lowered Ava down, so that the princess was straddling her. Ava sat on Liadan, her soft thighs hugging the bigger woman's hard body, and she appeared breathless, her big breasts lifting gently with her excitement, her lashes fluttering.

"You're so s-strong," the princess whispered, smoothing her little hands up and down Liadan's bulging arms.

"And you're so wet," Liadan whispered back. She could feel it, the hot moisture sliding from the princess' sex and onto her woolen hose. She looked down at the curly nest of golden hair between the young woman's thighs and saw how it glistened. Hunger stirred in her.

"I—I . . ." Princess Ava's lashes fluttered in embarrassment.

Liadan absently touched Ava's face, pushed the long golden hair back over her shoulder, thinking she was so soft and beautiful. "You were telling me what they say about my people," she said softly.

"They say you're aggressive and . . ." Ava looked down at Liadan and glanced over her body appreciatively. "I mean, you *were* a little aggressive last night, but it wasn't frightening as I thought it'd be."

Liadan had been stroking Ava's hair, but she looked quickly at the princess in concern. "You were afraid of me, my princess?"

"Not of you!" Ava said quickly. "Of . . . Well, I wondered if you might lose control of your strength when you were . . . touching me. I did not want my maidenhead to break and bleed." She smiled dotingly. "But you never did. You were rough . . . but you were gentle." She gazed off dreamily, remembering.

Liadan chuckled softly. "I am glad to see my princess is satisfied."

"So . . . can you do magick?" Ava asked, looking down at Liadan, hushed and excited. "Are the stories true?"

Liadan smiled, thinking Ava was like a little girl in so many ways. She had to remind herself that the princess had spent her entire life locked away at Caradin Castle, sheltered from all harm . . . and all life. She had probably never even seen magick.

Liadan lifted her hands, curving them as if she were cupping an invisible ball. She summoned the power until she could feel it running warm under her skin, and a second later, yellow fire had gathered between her hands in a ball, spinning and glowing, and reflected in Princess Ava's amazed green eyes like glass.

Ava's pink lips parted as she stared at the summoned yellow fire in awe. "Could I touch it?" she wondered innocently.

Liadan chuckled. "Only if you want to burn your fingers, your highness."

Ava bit her lip, no doubt feeling foolish.

Liadan let the light dissipate, breaking and falling away in a gold shower. She then carefully smoothed her hands over Ava's naked hips, knowing her touch was now pleasantly hot. Ava gasped in delight. Liadan continued caressing her, rubbing her strong hands up and down the princess' smooth skin, clutching at Ava's soft backside, sliding her hands up the deep line of the young woman's back. Ava's head fell back in delight, and she thrust her great breasts forward in response to Liadan's warm, gentle touch. Liadan sat up, and with blue eyes burning lust, she suckled roughly on Ava's pink nipple, until the great mound of her breast was swelling against her face, until the princess' helpless cries threatened to drift to the corridor.

Chapter 4

Lysa had to admit: she was a little bit jealous of Ava and Liadan. The next morning, as Liadan stood dutifully at the door in the corridor, Lysa brought the princess tea, and the two of them spoke for hours of Ava's first time with Liadan.

Ava was glowing and happy and couldn't contain her girlish excitement. And Lysa was happy for her. She sat, as ever, on a low footstool beside Ava's knee as Ava sat in the window seat, gazing dreamily out the arched window.

Lysa gazed up at Ava, thinking the princess was so beautiful. Ava loved pink, and that morning, she was draped in a long, near-translucent pink housecoat with a white nightgown beneath it. Her blonde hair hadn't been brushed by Lysa yet and was wild and untamed, falling over the cushions of the window seat and almost to the floor in golden curls. She took a sip of her tea, and for a moment, appeared sad.

"Liadan sounds too wonderful to be true," said Lysa with a happy sigh. She frowned. "But why do you look so glum, your highness?"

Ava looked around, and when she gazed down at Lysa, her green eyes were warm with affection. Lysa felt something in her thump.

"Haven't you ever been in love with someone you couldn't have?" said Ava heavily.

Lysa felt herself going pink. She was grateful when the princess didn't seem to notice and instead looked away out the window again.

"I think I'm in love with Liadan!" Ava breathlessly confessed. "But . . . I have to marry Prince Cassian. I'll have to lay with him and bear his children. And poor Liadan, she shall have to stand by and watch as I am bound in matrimony to another." She frowned. "It doesn't seem fair, does it? I want all the world to know I love her, but I couldn't even dance with her at the ball without a scandal."

"What if you ran away?" whispered Lysa with a hint of excitement, and she gripped Ava's knee, gazing eagerly up at her. In her girlish mind, Ava and Liadan were like something out of a fairytale. Their forbidden love was so . . . *romantic.* So she only expected them to follow the old tales and runaway. It was the only thing that made sense to her.

Ava looked down at Lysa in sad amusement, as if she were a silly little child. "Lysa!" she scolded. "I have a duty to the realm and to my house. I must remain here and marry, form the alliance, produce children . . ." She trailed off miserably.

"And be utterly wretched the rest of your life?" said Lysa in amazement. "You don't want a husband and children. You want Liadan!"

"Lysa . . ."

"Listen to me!" Lysa said over her. Ava looked down at Lysa sadly, and for the moment, all formality fell between them. They were not a princess and her servant gossiping over morning tea. They were two friends who had known each other since they were girls, who had shared everything, their joys and their sorrows.

"There will always be a war going on," said Lysa earnestly. "There will always be conquest, invasion, and the need for alliances. That is the way of men. They pillage and they rape and they kill! All men, from peasants to knights to kings! So why stay here, why give up your happiness to birth sons and further the legacy of men? Why not live for yourself?"

Ava gazed off in thought, her pale lashes blinking slowly. "I don't know, Lysa," she said after a while, and she sounded small and frightened, like the young child Lysa remembered sleeping beside when they were small.

"If I ran away, I could never return," Ava went on. "I would never see my father again. And Caradin, it's my home. I like living here."

"If you marry the prince of Almara, you'll have to leave with him. Only your sons shall return here to rule," Lysa pointed out.

Ava's lip trembled. "You're r-right, of course. But I just don't think I'm that brave. I've never been beyond the castle walls!"

Lysa gazed up at Ava in pity: there were tears behind the princess' green eyes. She stroked Ava's knee to calm her.

"Forget I said anything, fool that I am," Lysa said soothingly. "Here.. ." She rose to her feet and took the teacup from Ava. "Let's get you ready for breakfast with your father. He's waiting for you!"

PRINCESS AVA ALWAYS took breakfast and supper with her father in his solar, while having her noon meal alone in her room. It had become their custom over the years. They dined alone, without Lysa nearby and with the guards out in the hall, out of earshot. And so it was that Princess Ava went alone to break her fast with her father that morning, dressed in yet another beautiful pink gown, her long blonde hair falling in rippling, gold tresses to the small of her back, a delicate gold tiara upon her head.

The solar in the west wing of the castle overlooked the courtyard and the great garden below, its winter flowers now layered in white snow. The room was simple enough: stone walls and wood paneled floors, with red and gold tapestries hanging on the walls and standing gold candelabra. Before the fire was a bear rug and two cushioned chairs, and nestled in an alcove of arched windows was a small wooden table with two wooden chairs, elaborately carved. The king was already seated at the table and waiting, strapped in full golden armor, morning sunlight streaming across his golden, gray-streaked hair.

"How now, daughter!" said King Eyvor merrily the moment Ava glided into the room. He rose from his chair and paused in surprise when he beheld her face. "You look radiant!" he cried, as if he had never quite seen his daughter before. "In fact, I do believe you're glowing! Could it be you are excited for the arrival of your soon-to-be husband?"

Ava blushed hard and angled her pale lashes down. Her father thought she was excited about Prince Cassian while her mind was aflutter with ceaseless thoughts of Liadan. She had been forced to leave Liadan behind and wondered what the Knight of the Wild was doing at that very moment. Was she thinking of Ava? Was she wanting her?

Realizing her father was still staring at her in delight and amazement, Ava smiled and went to him, receiving an enthusiastic kiss on the cheek. They then sat together and broke their fast, as birds chirruped beyond the windowpane.

That morning, the table was covered in dishes and bowls of boiled eggs, kippered herring, and bread. Ava started filling her plate. So did her father.

"How do you like your new bodyguard?" King Eyvor asked – so suddenly that Ava nearly dropped her egg. She recovered quickly enough and answered, "V-Very well, Father. She is very . . . dutiful."

And strong and beautiful and good with her tongue, Ava thought dreamily. When she looked up again, her father was watching her curiously. She quickly lowered her eyes and took a sip of watered wine. By the *gods,* she was a bad liar. She prayed he didn't suspect her.

"You are in a strange mood this fine morn," said her father, still watching her closely. Eventually, he returned to his plate (to Ava's great relief). "Must be nerves. Do not worry. I was nervous when I met your mother, but then I looked in her eyes . . . and I knew."

Ava listened wistfully to her father and wondered if Liadan felt that way about her.

"The prince will love thee, make no mistake," went on the king merrily. "He will be here in another few weeks, I think. Him and his brother. There was a raven this morning. The traveling party is very close to the capital. Managed to carve their way past Bjorn's army easily enough. Elric always did have to show off." He snorted a laugh and pushed a boiled egg in his mouth whole.

Ava looked at her father in surprise. So it was true: Almara's armies *were* as strong as they had always claimed. Now she was seeing more than ever why an alliance with Almara was important, and when her father looked back at her, she knew he hadn't mentioned the strength of King Elric's armies without reason.

"I know my duty, Father," said Ava, solemnly spearing a herring slice on her fork. "I shall marry Prince Cassian and produce many strong sons." But even as Ava was saying the words, they tasted sour in her mouth, and she remembered what Lysa had said to her: in upholding the alliance and producing sons, she was only continuing the cycle of violence . . . the violence of men.

"Of course, you shall," said the king, very pleased. "You're my daughter! You understand the importance of duty."

"And what of the witch of the eastern wood?" asked Ava curiously. "If King Elric's army has already advanced so closely, surely, they had to cross her river. They had to pay a toll, didn't they?"

"Yes," said King Eyvor darkly. He sneered. "Magick! It should only belong in the hands of warriors! The Wildoras, they have it right. They use their power to aid the other realms! But creatures like that old Godga . . . she hath no honor."

Ava didn't answer and instead speared more sliced herring on her fork and slid it in her mouth. She knew the *real* reason her father suspected magick was because he didn't think women should wield it. Yet women alone had the ability, for magi were born, not made. Her father, like most of the men Ava knew, deeply resented this fact and only seemed to trust the sorceresses of Wildoras specifically because they were warriors and not pure magi.

"What toll do you think they paid, Father?" Ava prompted. The king looked so irritated that she was beginning to regret that she had brought up magick, but she was sincerely curious.

King Eyvor waved a hand. "The usual. Creatures like Godga always want one of two things: blood or babes."

Ava's face scrunched up. "Ghastly! What would she do with either?"

King Eyvor smiled affectionately at Ava. "Sweet child," he said dotingly, "I will not mar your innocence this day. No, that honor shall belong to Prince Cassian, your new husband!" He laughed and chose another boiled egg from the bowl.

Ava sneered, thinking the joke was in poor taste. How could her father laugh about the prince bedding her?! Especially when it was against her will? He might as well have been laughing about her rape.

King Eyvor seemed to believe Ava's disgust was with the prince and said with another dismissive wave, "I know they call him 'Princess Cassian' as a sort of jest, and tis true, the boy is a little. . . *effeminate.*" The king shook his head in stern disapproval. "But by the gods, he will do his duty by you or suffer the combined wraths of myself and his father!" He chuckled again and slid another boiled egg into his mouth, chewing happily behind his golden beard.

Ava sighed and poked at her plate with her fork. The *real* reason she had asked about the Magi Godga was to learn how to broker passage across the river. Lysa had put the idea in her head that she should run away, and the idea was looking more and more appealing the longer her father continued merrily ranting about her duty to lie with the prince.

So Magi Godga would ask for blood or children. Ava obviously didn't have any children and never intended to. Perhaps she could barter her blood. She was royalty, after all. Her house was ancient. Her blood had to be worth *something.*

"Mmm," said the king, still looking very amused by his own threats against Prince Cassian, "pass me the bread, would you, darling? Like a good girl?"

Marry a man and be raped by him, darling? Like a good girl? Ava thought viciously. "Of course, Father," she sighed and passed the bread basket.

Chapter 5

Weeks went by at Castle Caradin, and as the snow thickened on the castle walls, the heat between Princess Ava and Knight Liadan only seemed to grow ever more intense. Lysa had never intruded on the two in the act of lovemaking and indeed had made many excuses to give the pair privacy. She enjoyed seeing her princess happy, even if Ava couldn't be happy with her.

Lysa had been Princess Ava's handmaiden since they were both children, and as a result, had loved her since they were both children. They had always been inseparable. They would play Hide-and-Seek in the garden, pretend to siege fortresses under tent forts, share noon meals, even sleep in the same bed. When Ava was sad, Lysa was there to comfort her. When Ava was happy, Lysa was there to rejoice in her happiness.

Years and years of loyalty and diligent care, and Princess Ava had never loved Lysa back. She had kissed her once when they were sixteen, but Lysa doubted the princess even remembered it. Ava had drunk too much wine at a feast, and her furious father had sent her to bed early for it. As Lysa was tucking the drunken princess in, Ava had kissed her on the mouth, tongue and all, and had even whispered her name with a sort of husky desire. And though Lysa had gently rebuffed the princess' drunken advances, it was still the best night of Lysa's life.

Now Ava had finally found love, it seemed, and with her bodyguard. Lysa tried not to be jealous and instead supported Ava, helping the two find moments to be alone. For Lysa was terrified: if Ava and Liadan were discovered, they would be executed. And while Lysa wasn't entirely certain the king would behead his own daughter, she was more than completely convinced Liadan would be heading to the chopping block if she was caught with her hand down the princess' panties.

Lysa didn't wish for either to be harmed. She loved Princess Ava, and she liked Liadan a great deal. Liadan wasn't like the other knights, who constantly cursed Lysa for being underfoot or made lewd and crude passes at her. For a woman with noble blood, Liadan was down-to-earth, considerate, and kind – despite the fact that she was often broody and serious. And so, Lysa made certain to help in any way she could, keeping people away when she thought the two were at it, making excuses for the princess when her father was looking for her. And on it went for two weeks.

It was the middle of the third week when Prince Cassian and his father, King Elric, were due to arrive at Castle Caradin for a grand ball. Most of the king's council thought it absurd that the king should throw a ball in the middle of a war, but King Eyvor insisted that the kingdom needed a little happiness, and the announcement of a wedding – and thus an ally to aid in the war – would provide just that.

And so, Castle Caradin was abustle with servants running back and forth, covered in flour, preparing decorations, cooking roast meats, wheeling out cheeses and barrels of wine. The castle was in such chaos that no one noticed Princess Ava and Liadan's frequent and lengthy disappearances. Lysa was grateful for this, since she was kept so busy that she couldn't have covered for them anyway: all servants were expected to help in preparing for the ball, even the handmaiden of the princess.

Lysa was running down to the kitchen with grease fat for the cook when two stern guards blocked her path. Like all the guards in Caradin Castle, they were buckled in silver armor and were wearing green cloaks with the house sigil of Damaris on it: a single rose. They towered over Lysa, one a man, the other a woman, and their eyes in the darkness of their helms were narrow and cold slits. Lysa shrank beneath them and nearly dropped the grease fat.

"The king wishes to speak to you," said the woman harshly.

Lysa stammered out, "B-But why?"

"Does it matter?" snarled the man, impatient and disgusted. "When your king summons you, you obey!" So saying, the male knight smacked the jar of grease fat out of Lysa's hands (Lysa gasped in horror), and the two knights grabbed her by the arms and marched her away up the hall.

Lysa was trembling and terrified. In all her years serving in the castle, she had never once been summoned to the king! She had only ever been in his presence when accompanying Princess Ava, and then she had mostly been ignored. Now suddenly the king wanted to speak with her specifically? She wondered dismally if it didn't have something to do with Princess Ava and Knight Liadan.

They came to the war room where King Eyvor and his council often spent long hours bellowing at each other and bickering over strategy. Two knights were guarding the great wooden doors and nodded, pulling the doors open as they stepped aside. Lysa was marched by the grim knights into the room, where the king was sitting alone at a long table, upon which a great map of Realm Illa had been pinned with a dagger.

King Eyvor was in his full golden armor and had, in fact, started wearing his armor daily since the armies of Endoreth had drawn near the capital. His helm with the great red feather was on the table, and he was sipping a goblet of wine and looking very weary and resigned. He looked a great deal like his daughter: the same green eyes, the same blonde hair. Only there were gray streaks in his long blonde hair, and he was sporting a full beard that fell to his chest in a golden river of curls. Lysa had always thought the man looked magnificent and frightening, the way lions looked magnificent and frightening.

Glancing up and seeing Lysa there, the king gestured lazily for the guards to leave. The knights obeyed, releasing Lysa's arms and turning from the room. The great wooden doors closed gently behind them, and then Lysa found herself standing in the war room alone with the king, facing him meekly as he grimly stared her down. Behind him on the wall were great green banners bearing the rose sigil of House Damaris.

King Eyvor set down his goblet, fixed Lysa with a calm stare, and said without emotion, "I know of my daughter's tryst with the knight."

Lysa froze. She was afraid to confirm what had been happening, for perhaps it was a bluff. But to deny that it was happening to the king's face? She could be run through with a sword for such deception. So she stood there and said nothing.

The king seemed to understand Lysa's dilemma and smiled sadly. "Your loyalty to my daughter is touching. I know you have loved her long these years, and that you have suffered in silence."

Lysa's mouth fell open. "Your majesty, I n-never—!"

"Oh, I know you never lay with my daughter," said the king, waving a dismissive hand. "And even if you had, I would care not. You're a handmaiden, not a knight or a noblewoman. There would be no political outrage should you have bedded my daughter. But this woman who I was fool enough to bring here, this Liadan . . . She could pose a threat to the alliance with Almara. She is trained to kill, and the blood that runs through her veins is that of the First People. Magick blood. Ancient blood. And she will be forced to watch as my daughter is wed to a man, as that man touches my daughter and woos her. She might react in anger. The rage-blood runs deep in the people of the wild, no matter how calm Liadan might appear on the surface."

Lysa knew where the king was going: he was terrified Liadan would attack Prince Cassian, and then there would be no alliance between their kingdoms . . . and then Realm Illa would fall, alone in the fight against Endoreth.

"Now, don't misunderstand, child," went on the king reassuringly. "I have no ill will toward women who love other women. Ava is my child, my only child, and I love her, the gods be damned. But now is not the time for her to run wild like her grandmother! Avaria had her little trysts during a time of peace. Ava cannot say the same. She has a duty to the realm and to her house. To protect the alliance with Almara, this affair with the knight must end." The king paused, gazing meaningfully at Lysa.

Lysa felt the misery welling up inside her. She did not want to play a role in breaking Ava and Liadan apart. Ava would never forgive her, and what would happen to Liadan? Murder? Exile? She looked at the king in sadness and fear.

"Do not be afeared, girl," the king said gently. "I will not harm Liadan. I respect the people of Wildoras too greatly. And she has done me a service, guarding my child these last few weeks. Did you know assassins did try to end Ava's life only the week before? That Liadan slew them in the night like rats? Singlehandedly."

Lysa raised her brows in surprise. She had not known that.

"The girl is easily the greatest bodyguard I could have asked for," went on the king, "which is why I cannot allow her to ruin her own life and the life of my daughter by attacking Prince Cassian. By removing Liadan, I can protect her life. I would be forced to execute her to appease the Almari otherwise. You understand?"

Lysa nodded dismally and bowed her head. She understood: in order to protect Ava, she would have to lose her friendship. Ava would never forgive her for taking away Liadan, the first and only woman she had ever loved. But if it meant protecting Ava, then Lysa must grit her teeth and do it.

Lysa lifted her head again, and she could see the king watching her. He appeared satisfied to see her sudden resolve.

"What must I do, your majesty?" Lysa asked with confidence.

The king smiled. "That's the spirit, child. That's the spirit."

Chapter 6

Princess Ava couldn't imagine where Liadan was. The knight had been summoned to the courtyard by Captain Kenric, and Ava hadn't seen her since. What was more, Lysa was behaving very strangely. She was more nervous and anxious than ever, often fumbling over Ava's laces and hair as she helped her get dressed for the ball that evening.

Ava was miserable. She stood facing her tall golden mirror as Lysa laced her into her magnificent pink gown, thinking that she looked beautiful with her cascading hair and swelling cleavage, and Liadan wouldn't be there to see it. How she had looked forward to Liadan's reaction, to the hunger in her eyes! She had not been looking forward to meeting her future husband, but the thought of having Liadan there with her had at least made the idea bearable. Now she didn't even have the small comfort of her love at her side.

"Perhaps she left on purpose, to avoid seeing you with the prince," suggested Lysa meekly. She paused, brush in hand, hairpins sticking from her fist, and looked up at Ava hopefully, as if desperate to sooth her.

"Liadan would never leave my side!" Ava insisted, almost tearful. "Not even out of envy! No, something must've happened to her! I asked Father, the council, and half the guard, but everyone is acting as if it doesn't matter and—!" Ava halted when she noticed Lysa's reflection in the mirror. A look of guilt had crossed Lysa's face, a look that came and went so quickly, Ava wasn't supposed to have seen it, but she did.

Ava whirled and grabbed Lysa roughly by the shoulders – so suddenly and so fiercely, Lysa screamed softly and dropped the brush and hairpins.

"You know something!" Ava accused.

Lysa dismally shook her head. "My princess – Eep!" she shrieked when Ava gave her a little shake.

"What do you know? Tell me!" Ava demanded.

Lysa bowed her head. "I . . . locked you in your bedchamber while they took Liadan away."

Ava stared, caught somewhere between shock and fury. "That was you?"

Lysa nodded dismally. "I wasn't going to tell you. I didn't want you to h-hate me—"

"You lied to me. You told me the handle was broken! And while I was shut away in here, what were they doing to her – Speak!" She shook Lysa again, and the quivering little maid squeaked like a mouse that had been stepped on.

"They didn't *harm* her, your highness!" Lysa insisted wretchedly. "They just . . . sent her away."

Ava scowled. "Why?"

Lysa swallowed hard, her frightened eyes full of tears. "Your father was afeared that Liadan would become jealous at the ball and attack the prince, so he had her sent from the castle for the night. Though . . . though I don't think she'll be allowed back. I heard him talking of replacing her . . . with a man."

Ava absently released Lysa's shoulders and stood there, staring into space. She felt as if someone had punched the breath out of her. For several seconds, she couldn't move. Just the day before, she had lain in bed with Liadan, kissing her, whispering with her, giggling at her teasing, and had fallen asleep in her strong arms. And now, she had just been told that she would never know Liadan's arms again. Never see her smile. Or feel her soft kisses.

Tears rose to blind Ava.

"My princess . . ." Lysa whispered miserably.

"Don't you *dare* call me that!" Ava snarled, her voice a sob. She looked up through a veil of tears and could see Lysa watching her miserably. The little handmaiden looked so defeated.

Ava turned to the doors. "I'm going down to the ball, and you shall stay here. When I have returned, you will have packed your things and left Caradin—"

"Princess!" Lysa gasped.

"—and I never want to see you again," Ava said darkly and marched from the room. As she slammed the doors behind her, she thought she heard Lysa sobbing hard.

Chapter 7

Ethne Cawthorne was often called the Knight of the Sparrow for the sigil of her house. She was a beautiful knight with dark brown hair pulled back in a messy bun and gray eyes wreathed in thick lashes. She was not quite as tall as Liadan nor as a strong, not being from Realm Wildoras, but she was a hearty and strong woman nonetheless, an Illa native and from a very old and well-respected noble house.

And so, it goes without saying that Ethne had always been a little jealous of Liadan, who came from the wild country and yet garnered much respect and difference at the academy almost immediately, while Ethne was a damn native who had worked twice as hard for her shield and yet still bore the shame of having been disowned by her own family.

How bitter and seething was Ethne when Liadan was chosen – by the king himself!—to become the guardian of the princess. Not even a native of Illa and given such an honor! All the knights at the academy, however, had envied Liadan, not just Ethne. The princess was the most beautiful woman in the realm, the stories said, and many suspected she possessed the hot blood of her loose and wild grandmother to boot. There had been talk for years of the princess bedding the castle guards, running wild, and driving her poor father mad, and so it was believed that anyone who guarded her would have been invited between her thighs rather quickly.

How disappointed, then, was Ethne when Liadan turned up in the tavern on the verge of tears, ranting on about how the princess was a virgin, innocent and sweet, and how she had fallen in love with her, only for the princess to send her forth from the castle for fear of "offending" her future husband, the prince.

Liadan was inconsolable, blubbering incoherently over her tankard of ale. Ethne had never seen her cry before that evening. She dragged her friend to a corner table to avoid drawing attention to them, but Liadan wouldn't cease her loud sobbing. She was a mess. Ethne found it both exasperating and painful to watch.

"Pull yourself together or we shall be booted out," Ethne begged, her eyes moving anxiously over the many annoyed faces that kept turning their way. The barkeep in particular looked grumpy, for her patrons were trying to enjoy the evening with drink and dance, but Liadan was disrupting the fun with her loud crying.

Sighing, Ethne passed Liadan a kerchief, at the same time taking her ale. The woman had had enough for one night.

A little tipsy but not full-out drunk, Liadan sniffled and mopped her face with the kerchief. She was disheveled, her red hair flying, her face streaked with tears. Ethne watched her in sympathy.

"So the princess is a virgin," Ethne said thoughtfully. "That's surprising given her family history."

"She's not a virgin any longer," said Liadan meaningfully. She smiled through her tears, and Ethne shouted out a laugh.

Liadan's smile was fleeting, however. It fell almost immediately from her lips, and she stared dismally at the table.

"All the women you have bedded," Ethne said in wonder, "and *this* one has you in your cups? She must have one sweet honeypot for all of this." She shook her head in amazement.

Liadan scowled. "You dare! I'd ring your ears if I could but figure out which one of you was real."

Ethne laughed softly. "That I do not doubt. But tell me truly: what is so special about this one? I simply don't understand it. It'd almost be comical if you weren't such a hapless mess."

Liadan glared sideways at Ethne but obliged her, "I don't know how to make you understand. Ava is the woman for me. I looked in her eyes, and I knew, and that was that. Or at least . . . I thought I knew." She glared into the distance. "My lady had me sent forth from the castle to please that snotty fop, Prince Cassian. Without so much as a fare thee well!"

"How do you know that is true, though?" Ethne pointed out. "Just because Captain Kenric told you it was so? The man despises you. Why believe him?"

Liadan waved a disgusted hand. "Why shouldn't I believe him? Ava was always on about her duty to the realm and how she was afraid we would be discovered."

"And yet, she kept spreading her legs, the way you tell it," said Ethne dismissively.

Liadan glared. "Do not jest! My love has cast me out, and all you can do is jest!"

"And you deserve it," said Ethne sternly. "What you did was foolhardy."

Liadan glared again. "Are you on my side or not?"

Ethne shrugged, unabashed. "You would have cast aside your honor and reputation – your *life*—for a woman you couldn't have! Have you learnt nothing from my wretched life? Had Ava's father caught you in the act, you would have been publicly executed, Liadan. Executed! Perhaps she sent you forth to spare you from that, and she sent the guards with lies to keep you away. She likely assumed you would return anyway, even while knowing the danger, stubborn fool that you are." Ethne laughed. "Your lady knows you well after only three weeks of bliss, I'll give her that. The two of you must've done more than just tongue-fucking then."

Liadan laughed as well, though it was more a half-hearted and empty sound. With a sudden wave of sympathy, Ethne reached over and patted Liadan gently on her gauntlet. Envy the red knight though she did, Liadan was still her sister in arms and always would be.

Ethne was about to attempt some comforting words when the tavern doors opened and swung shut again. She looked over and went still: a very lovely young woman had just entered the room. She was a little meek and frightened, very small – barely five feet tall – and slender, with small breasts that stood nonetheless ripe behind her simple servant's gown. Her brown hair was shoulder-length and unremarkable, and her round face was almost plain, though the flush on her cheeks made her fresh and appealing, and her pink lips gave her a sweet innocence, as did her imploring brown eyes.

The peasant girl simply stood in the doorway like one frozen, gazing around as if in search of someone. Many heads in the noisy tavern turned her way, and a few peasant men paused in their drinking and laughing to stare at the girl, eyes glazed with lust. Ethne's muscles tightened in fear for the young woman – fear and anger. Would they dare attempt something on that sweet girl in the middle of the tavern, with a knight sitting nearby? The gall! Her hand instinctively went to her sword hilt under the table, and her muscles remained tight.

"Are you going to drink that?" Liadan slurred, streams of red hair in her wet eyes.

Ethne looked around: Liadan had taken her pint and was drinking from it. She snatched the pint from Liadan's hand (Liadan moaned in complaint) and turned her attention back to the young peasant girl.

"Who is that maiden? The one at the door. She is quite fair and clean-faced . . . for a peasant," said Ethne, gazing intently at the young woman across the room.

Liadan snorted in amusement. "You are of noble blood, but your house has dismissed you, least you forget. You are not in a position to call anyone a peasant anymore, my haughty friend."

Ethne felt a bubble of anger rising but ignored Liadan. The peasant woman's eyes had found them, and to her surprise, the young woman's gaze connected with Ethne's. To Ethne's amazement, the peasant glanced indifferently over the sparrow sigil on Ethne's armor, then her eyes went to Liadan and filled with relief. She hurried to their table, pushing through the other tables, which were crowded for the supper meal. A drunk man made a swipe at the woman's breasts and missed. She blushed miserably and moved faster.

Liadan looked up from the table and went still. "By the gods . . . *Lysa?* What are you doing in such a place? And alone? You could be harmed!" She reached out, grabbed Lysa's arm, and gently pulled her down on the chair beside her – forcing Lysa to sit opposite Ethne.

Lysa staggered as she was pulled near, tripped, and sat hard, her little breasts bouncing. Ethne couldn't help watching Lysa's breasts and felt a little guilty when Lysa glared at her and crossed her arms over them. But there was hesitance in Lysa's eyes, and her pink lips turned in a small smile: she liked Ethne's staring. Ethne smiled back.

"What are you doing here?" Liadan repeated, and she sounded like a scolding mother. "The place is filled with drunken brutes who will not hesitate to grope and molest—"

"And if any one of them dares, I shall have to cut their hand off," growled Ethne, who had noticed a few peasant men watching them from the bar. When she looked around again, she found Lysa watching her with round-eyed admiration. The girl blushed when their eyes connected again.

"Who is your friend?!" Lysa gasped, looking around at Liadan. She was breathless and caught in a sort of trance as she turned her eyes back to Ethne, who was enjoying her doting.

"I am Ethne, my lady," said Ethne before Liadan could answer. "Ethne of House Cawthorne. I am known as the Knight of the Sparrow."

The apparent Lysa blinked, then as if embarrassed by her own amazement, she turned her eyes back to Liadan. "I am h-here because Ava dismissed me," she admitted sadly, and Ethne realized for the first time that she was clutching a little knapsack of her belongings. Her hair was also tousled and messy as if from distress, and her face was streaked with dried tears. She looked at the table with a trembling lip. "I have nowhere to g-go. I have lived in the castle since I was five. They bought me from my mother for five gold crowns."

Liadan frowned in sympathy. "Ah. So the cold-hearted wench has cast you out as well, has she? You are welcome to travel with us, if you like. Ethne is a good sort – for the most part—"

Ethne laughed. "Piff. What would you do without me, Liadan?" she teased. "I am always saving your arse."

"—and shall not harm you," Liadan went on irritably, "though she shall likely attempt at your skirt. No young maiden is safe in her presence."

Lysa blushed brightly and avoided Ethne's eye.

"We are heading to the Temple of Eyslath in Hastow, there to become knights in service of the goddess," added Ethne, hoping for Lysa to turn her pretty eyes back her way. "I'm sure the temple could use a servant. They take peasants of all sorts."

Lysa stiffened indignantly, and Ethne knew at once that she had put her foot in her mouth. She ignored Liadan's laughing eyes and reached across the table, gently taking Lysa's little hand in her gauntlet. "I must confess, it would be a waste, a woman as pretty as thee—"

Lysa snatched her hand free. "A peasant, you mean!" she shrilled.

Ethne's mouth dropped open and she mouthed silently a moment. "I . . . I only meant—"

"I don't care what you meant!" Lysa snapped and returned her attention to Liadan, who was looking very amused by the exchange. Defeated, Ethne sat back and glared at Liadan, who kept smiling but didn't dare say a word.

"I have come about Ava," said Lysa, gazing at Liadan imploringly.

Liadan's face immediately darkened. "I care not to discuss her."

Lysa shook her head. "Liadan, *listen* to me! Ava didn't send you away! That was a lie!"

Liadan hesitated. "What trickery is this?"

"If this is a trick, it is a poor one," said Lysa impatiently. "The king asked me to bring Ava into her bedchamber and lock her in so that . . . so that he could send you away without an in-incident . . ." Her voice trembled to silence as Liadan glared down at her from her great height, the wild red hair blazing around her like fire.

"Without you slaying half the guard, she means," said Ethne, amused.

"So we were parted with lies and deceit," said Liadan darkly, "and you – you played a part in it! And now you come here to what? Assuage your guilt now that Ava hath rightfully sent you forth?"

Lysa sighed miserably, and Ethne knew exactly how she felt: Liadan could be a stubborn fool at the worst of times.

"Liadan, listen to her, for the sake of the gods," said Ethne irritably. "She obviously didn't part you from the princess willingly!"

Liadan grudgingly turned her eyes back to Lysa, and Ethne was glad to see some of the anger had softened from them. "So why then have you come?" Liadan asked calmly, though there was still a note of bitterness in her voice.

"Ava loves you," Lysa said at once, "and I love Ava!"

Something in the young woman's words stung Ethne. She had the immediate feeling Lysa loved Ava as more than a friend. She wasn't too bothered, however. It only meant she would have to work harder for Lysa's affections, and she liked a challenge.

"I want Ava to be happy, and she would be miserable with Prince Cassian," went on Lysa. "Helping the king was a mistake, I know that now. I didn't have a *choice*," she added bitterly before Liadan could berate her, "and now I have come to rectify the mistake, if only you would listen."

"So what do you suggest?" said Liadan, waving a dismissive gauntlet. "That the three of us storm the castle and take Ava by force?"

"Have you been *listening* to me?" Lysa demanded. "I've worked in the castle since I was five! I know all the secret passages inside and out! I can get you in without bloodshed, and if we are caught, well . . . You're a magi, for the sake of the gods. The king told me how you slew those assassins who came for Ava."

"Hmm," said Ethne thoughtfully. "The lass makes sense. With my help, and with her knowledge of the passages, we might be able to steal the princess away." She placed a gauntlet on Liadan's arm. "But consider it carefully, good Liadan. We shall be exiled from Illa, never to return. I know we were heading for Hastow either way, but . . . are you willing to give up everything you are and everything you have for Ava?"

Liadan looked at Ethne helplessly as she said, "Everything I am and everything I have is already hers."

Chapter 8

The ball was the same boring affair as every ball Princess Ava had ever attended, only this time she was spared the agony of having to endure an endless line of male suitors and their flirting. Instead, she was expected to spend the night on Prince Cassian's arm, listening to his jokes and attempting to get to know her future husband. Just thinking of the prospect, she almost wanted the annoying male suitors back.

Four thrones had been placed at the end of the ballroom at the top of the dais, as behind them hung the green banners of House Damaris and its rose sigil. Ava and her father sat on the two center thrones as Prince Cassian and his father were announced. The prince approached the throne up the avenue of murmuring on-lookers, chin lifted, and bowed before Ava where she sat, politely kissing her hand. Ava was surprised by how cold the kiss was, and when the prince sat beside her without even looking at her, it quickly occurred to her that he had no desire to be there any more than she did.

Prince Cassian was a handsome young man close to Ava's years. Like all Almarans, he was dark in his aspect, with jet-black hair and dark, hawk-like eyes. He was smooth shaven, which gave him a boyish appearance, and he wore a great deal of jewelry, an elaborately embroidered tunic, and very fine leather boots. The handsome prince, peacock that he was, almost outshone Ava in his splendor, something many of the courtiers twittered about behind fans.

The two kings sat either side their children on their thrones, talking loudly of the joyous union to be had. Eventually, King Eyvor kissed Ava's cheek (she smiled briefly under the affection), then he and King Elric rose (the music stopped abruptly and everyone bowed) and retired to the balcony, where they stood smoking, sipping goblets, and speaking in grave undertones. Near the kings, an accompaniment of knights in green cloaks stood guard.

As soon as the kings had set foot on the balcony, the music picked up again, and the guests returned to their dancing, the men spinning the women in their long gowns around the floor. Everyone looked so happy, laughing and carrying on, clapping, dancing, drinking. Ava looked down at them from her throne and felt like an outsider looking in. Then she glared after her father, whose back was to her as he stood on the balcony.

After Lysa's frantic confession, Ava now knew that her father had sent Liadan away and that her knight hadn't, in fact, abandoned her. She wanted to be angry with King Eyvor, but she knew deep down that he had done it for her own good. Perhaps Lysa had told him what was happening between her and Liadan, and wanting to spare Liadan the chopping block, her father had sent the Knight of the Wild away.

Lysa! It had to have been her! How else could her father have known? She and Liadan had been so careful. . . hadn't they? But why? Was Lysa jealous? Ava had suspected for years that Lysa desired her, but she had never believed her capable of such betrayal! Tears almost rose to blind her, and she angrily pushed them down. She would die happy if she never saw Lysa again!

Left to their own devices, Ava and Prince Cassian sat on their thrones in silence, watching the dancing. Ava tried not to think of Liadan, but the knight was ever at the back of her mind. She wished Liadan was there and wondered where she was, what she was doing, if she was thinking of her as well. But even if Liadan was there at that very moment, she and Ava couldn't have participated in the dancing and the fun. Not as a couple. Even if Liadan had been there, they would have remained a hidden secret, a secret shame. Ava watched the dancers with bitter envy and almost hatred, knowing that she would never have the chance to dance with Liadan at a grand ball, openly kiss her or hold her hand, even marry her with a great, beautiful wedding! And all for the sake of the alliance!

In some twisted way, King Bjorn's invasion of Realm Illa had indirectly ruined Ava's love life.

"Are you well, dear princess?"

Ava looked around and was embarrassed – and a little surprised – to find Prince Cassian watching her with concern.

"You look ill," he said, frowning. "Do you need air?" He offered his kerchief, the many gold rings on his slender fingers sparkling.

"Thank you," Ava whispered and took the kerchief, realizing for the first time that her face was streaked with tears.

"Come," said Prince Cassian, rising. "I grow weary of these affairs rather quickly anyway." He offered his arm.

Suddenly wanting to be as far from the happy dancers as possible, Ava took the prince's arm and allowed him to help her stand. As they stepped gracefully down from the dais, the music stopped, and heads rippled down as the crowds bowed. There was silence until Ava and Prince Cassian had disappeared into the hall, and then the music picked up and the dancing continued. The laughter echoed behind them as they went, and Ava was glad to put distance between herself and the ballroom. She could not bear watching others laugh and dance while she was weighed down with longing for Liadan.

"Where shall we go?" Prince Cassian asked Ava as they walked down the torchlit corridor, along which knights in armor stood guard. "To the courtyard? I heard you had a lovely garden, even in the winter."

"Yes, let's," agreed Ava. "I do believe I need some air after all."

They sent servants to fetch their fur cloaks, and out they went.

Outside, darkness had fallen, and the stars winked over the stone courtyard, bright against the inky blue sky. Many of the flowers were white night-bloomers, and they stood with their petals open in the moonlight, rising almost defiant from caps of snow.

"Exquisite," the prince said when he saw the flowers. "Simply marvelous. What are they?"

"We call them Moon flowers, dear prince," answered Ava.

"Moon flowers," said the prince softly, gazing around with a sort of hushed awe. "Lovely."

Ava's brows went up in surprise. "Does his highness have an interest in flowers?"

"Don't be silly. A man may like flowers," said the prince dismissively.

"Yes," said Ava, holding back a smile, "but most men wouldn't advertise it."

The prince's lips twisted in an odd half-smile. "I am not most men. Shall we sit?"

They came to a stone bench and sat side by side. The courtyard was still and the air crisp and cold in the silent and gentle snowfall. Ava was wearing a winter gown with long sleeves lined in fur, but still, she felt the icy bite of the wind. She pulled her fur cloak tighter around her shoulders, silently grateful for the breeze that combed cold fingers through her hair. A moment before, she had felt feverish and ill.

"You know, I didn't want to come here tonight," admitted the prince after a pause.

"I noticed," said Ava with a short laugh. "You were rather brief and distant back in the ballroom."

"Was I? I apologize. It's just . . . I cannot consent to this marriage. My mind consents. I know my duty, and I will do what I must for my country's sake. But my heart . . . My heart shall never fully submit. I am incapable of loving you, I must confess. It wouldn't be fair to pretend otherwise."

Ava frowned, looking at the prince steadily. "What do you mean?"

The prince took a shaking breath. "I mean that my heart belongs to my bodyguard—"

Ava went still.

"—a man a few years my senior, assigned to me by my father—"

Ava couldn't stop herself: she burst out laughing. The prince stared at her, tight-lipped and angry, but she couldn't help herself: she laughed and laughed and laughed. When she had finally sighed herself to silence, the prince folded his arms and sneered, "If you can't sit with me and have a mature conversation—"

"No, no," said Ava, still sighing with laughter and shaking her head. "It's just that . . . I'm in love with my bodyguard as well."

The prince stared at her. "You're having me on."

"No," said Ava, laughing again. "Only my father has sent her away, to keep the two of you from fighting over me. And now it turns out you fancy men anyway. My life is one big jest." And she didn't know why, but she suddenly broke down sobbing into the kerchief.

"There, there," said the prince sadly, and Ava felt him patting her shoulder. "What a pair we make," he said with a sigh. "I love my lover and you love yours, and yet they would have us wed." He looked at Ava curiously. "What if we ran away?"

"Don't be foolish," said Ava at once. "Our countries need this alliance."

The prince waved an impatient hand. "Our fathers could unite and fight the Endorethi without our marriage. They are only doing this to join our houses, to ensure that one doesn't betray the other. They are selfish old men who would sacrifice our happiness for their futile war."

Ava looked at the prince, thinking in amazement that he sounded a great deal like Lysa.

"Be fair now," said Ava, frowning. "It isn't as if our fathers conjured all of this up to punish us. King Bjorn decided to go on his ridiculous crusade to conquer the seven kingdoms all on his own and without any help from our fathers."

"That is true," admitted the prince grudgingly, "but my point still stands. There is no real reason we should wed other than our fathers don't trust each other."

"There's no use complaining about it now. If we both fancy those of our own sex, then I don't see why our marriage must be so miserable. We could simply wed and not lay together."

"How do you figure that? We would be expected to produce an heir."

"I would need your seed to produce an heir, not you."

The prince laughed. "True enough, dearest princess. You know, I suspect we could be good friends, given time." He smiled at Ava, and Ava looked into his eyes, thinking they were kind eyes, like her father's.

"I don't see why not," agreed Ava. "You aren't nearly as insufferable as my suitors of the past."

The prince laughed heartily at that. "Yes, well, that's because I have no desire to get in your smallclothes."

"Thank the gods," said Ava wearily.

They laughed.

"Be glad I am the eldest and not my brother," said the prince. "Otherwise, you'd be enduring his searing wit and charm about now."

"Your brother?" repeated Ava curiously.

"Yes. Cristen. Thinks he's a real ladies' man. Doesn't take 'no' for an answer."

"Sounds like a prize," said Ava sarcastically.

The prince laughed. "Indeed. Shall we return to the ball?"

"Let's," agreed Ava. "I am suffering in this cold much more than I shall admit."

The prince laughed. He offered his arm, Ava took it, and they were about to stand when the prince gasped and went rigid, his eyes growing wide. Something wet splattered Ava's face, and the prince's arm, which had been tight and strong a moment before, slid from Ava's grasp.

Heart pounding in her ears, Ava slowly looked down and screamed: an arrow had sprouted from Prince Cassian's chest, sprouted from his heart. Dark blood was quickly spreading over his tunic, and his eyes – so full of laughter and life mere seconds before – were staring blankly as he sat, slumped back, on the stone bench.

Ava looked around and saw the archer seconds before she released another arrow – a woman was crouched on the wall above, dressed in black, her hood up, her eyes vicious slits in the darkness of the hood. Black licks of hair streamed from her hood on the wind, and Ava heard a soft rasp of laughter as she sent another arrow flying.

Ava screamed and threw herself out of the way. She fell down in the flowers, in the snow. From the corner of her eye, she saw the assassin leap from the wall and down into the courtyard, landing catlike in the snow.

"I only meant to wound you!" called the assassin in a taunting, sing-song voice.

"Guards!" Ava screamed as loudly as she could. There was no point trying to hide where she was: she was trailing Prince Cassian's blood in the snow, as well as her own footprints.

"The guards aren't coming," rasped the assassin, who was taking her time as she crossed the courtyard. She nocked another arrow and casually fired as she came.

Ava screamed and rolled frantically behind a stone statue. With Prince Cassian's blood still on her face, she scrambled up and pressed her back to the statue, heart racing, listening as the assassin came for her, boots crunching over the snow. A heavy stone was nearby, about the size of an apple, and Ava snatched it up and went still again, listening.

"I was sent to capture you alive," the assassin said, "so make this easy for us both and just come out, *princess*. Or," she nocked another arrow, "we can play Hide-and-Seek all night. That's fine. I've killed most of the guards. The others are half across the castle, and by the time they get here, we'll be gone."

Eyes down as she followed the marks in the snow, the assassin rounded the statue where Ava was hiding.

"No, we won't!" Ava yelled and leapt out of hiding, the stone raised to strike. She screamed in frustration when the assassin caught her swinging arm at the wrist, halting the fall of the stone. Her smiling eyes laughed at Ava – and then suddenly went wide.

Ava and the assassin slowly looked down: a sword had blossomed in the woman's stomach. Standing over the woman's shoulder was a young man who looked a great deal like Prince Cassian. He was tall and slender like his brother, with the same dark hair and eyes. He smiled at Ava over the assassin's shoulder and ripped the sword free. The assassin, staring blankly, fell forward to the ground in a toss of snow.

Breathless, breasts heaving, Ava felt the relief washing over her. "Prince Cristen," she said gratefully, for who else could it have been?

The prince smiled nastily, and stabbing the sword in the snow, he gave Ava a sarcastic bow, his arms outstretched. Ava went still: she did not like the mockery in his eyes.

"Fair Princess Ava," said Cristen, straightening up. "With my fool brother out of the way, you shall be mine. I have saved your life. Where are my kisses? Where are my accolades?"

Ava stood very still. Something was wrong here. "You . . . had your brother killed, didn't you?" she said wretchedly.

Prince Cristen smiled darkly. "Smarter than you look, I'll give you that. Most princesses navigate life with their tits." He glanced down. "And yours are magnificent, by the way." Like his brother, his hand was heavy with gold rings. It went to his belt, where a dagger was sheathed.

Ava heard her heart pounding in her ears, screaming a warning. She turned and ran, but the prince was quick: he grabbed a fistful of her golden hair and yanked her back, placing the dagger to her throat. Ava went very still, her heart still pounding, her breasts heaving with her breathlessness. She could feel the prince's breath on her ear as he whispered, "Be still now. I'm not going to hurt you. I just want to look at you. You're going to be my wife now, Ava. It doesn't matter if I see you naked now. If you scream, I'll slit your throat, and the alliance be damned. Understand?"

Ava nodded wretchedly.

"Good girl," Prince Cristen whispered.

Pass the bread like a good little girl, Ava thought, remembering breakfast with her father weeks before. *Lie still and be raped like a good little girl.* She was suddenly so tired of being a good little girl, but she couldn't hope to fight back. She was helpless against Cristen, helpless against the world. She hated herself for never learning to fight.

Ava went still when the dagger moved from her throat to the front of her gown. The prince dragged it over the fabric, and she watched in silent horror as her gown slowly tore open, until the fabric was hanging loosely around her large naked breasts and trembling belly. Her nipples hardened at once in the cold, standing sharp from the plump mounds of her flesh. She heard the prince sigh with longing and could taste the sick at the back of her throat when his erection hit the back of her skirt through his trousers.

The prince sheathed his dagger. "By the *gods,*" he whispered, pulling slightly on her hair, so that her head tilted back and her big breasts were lifted higher. Ava blazed with anger at this. "Release me!" she hissed.

"No," said Prince Cristen. "I think I'll have a squeeze. Your tits are just too luscious to resist—"

"No!" Ava whispered, horrified. "Please—!" She rolled her eyes down and watched, paralyzed with terror, as the prince's hand reached for one of her breasts—but the prince never managed to successfully grope Ava. She heard him choke out a pained cry, then his fingers released her hair, and she heard him collapse to the snow.

Panting and clutching her breasts to hide them, Ava turned to face her rescuer: it was Liadan.

The Knight of the Wild's face was calm in her anger, the warpaint still swirling over her cheek and falling in streaks under her eye. Her red hair, wild and flying, was sprinkled with blood and snow, and snow clung to her lashes as she glared at the body at her feet. Ava looked down at the body as well and gasped: Liadan had cut off Cristen's head.

Liadan's blazing blue eyes went to Ava and softened in concern. "Are you all right, my princess? Did he hurt you?"

"You came for me!" said Ava eagerly and was startled by her own bright happiness. It had only been a day, but it felt as if Liadan had been absent for a lifetime.

"I would never let a man touch your sweet body," Liadan said, gazing down at Ava intently.

Ava's heart was beating wild with excitement, and Liadan looked so beautiful standing there, so powerful and fierce, towering over her, sword in hand. She was glowing with golden light . . . with magick. And she was breathless and sweaty. She must've fought her way there. And she was hurt! Blood was trickling from Liadan's brow and from her arm.

"No! Your arm!" Ava whispered, drawing close. She placed a careful hand on Liadan's vambrace, wishing that she could bandage her at least. When she looked up again, Liadan was gazing down at her with soft-eyed affection, pleased by her concern.

"I came to take you from here," Liadan said breathlessly. She smiled sadly. "If my princess would still have me."

Ava looked in Liadan's warm blue eyes and something in her melted. She took the knight's gauntlet in both her hands and whispered happily, "Take me from here, and I shall follow you, my knight, throughout the world!"

Liadan smiled, and without warning, she snatched Ava close in the wall of her hard arm and kissed her passionately.

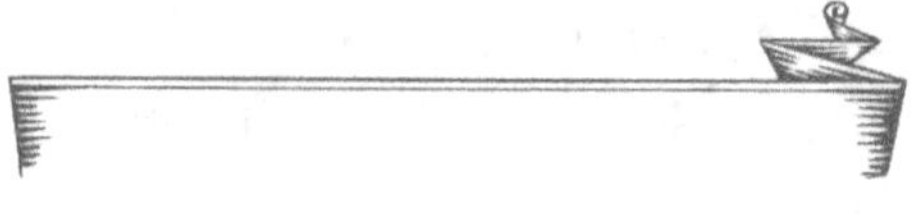

More From Ash Gray

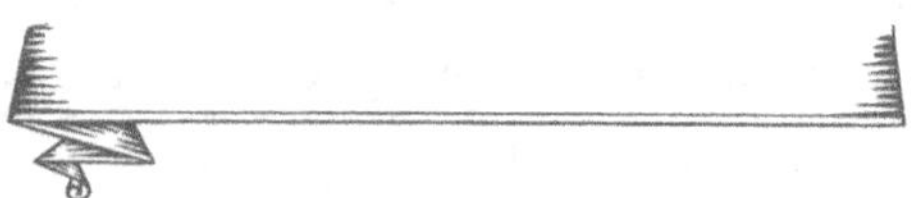

Her First Knight
Book 2
Sparrow Song
Chapter 1

Because Prince Cristen had ruined Ava's gown, Liadan took off her own fur cloak and wrapped it reverently around Ava. She then lifted the princess into her arms and turned back toward the castle, heading through a secret passage Ava recognized immediately. Ava knew before she even saw Lysa that it was Lysa who had helped Liadan: the Knight of the Wild hadn't been at Castle Caradin long enough to have learned all the secret passages, but Lysa would have known this one.

The passage led beyond the castle wall, to an empty field, where the snow fell over the frozen lake. Ava recognized it as the edge of her father's hunting grounds. In the distance, she could see the forest and how the snow capped the dark trees. It was quiet and serene here, as behind them, the bell rang frantic in the tower, men shouted and horns were blown: Prince Cassian and Prince Cristen (and the assassin) had been found dead in the courtyard, and Princess Ava's absence had been realized.

Lysa was waiting nearby, shivering in the snowfall, wearing a fur cloak over her simple gown and carrying a bundle in her arms. Beside her were two saddled horses, one white, the other brown, and beside the horses stood a knight Ava didn't recognize. When Liadan set Ava on her feet, the princess hesitated uncertainly.

The strange knight was tall and strong like Liadan, beautiful, with fiercely slanted gray eyes, and on the front of her beautifully engraved silver breastplate was the sigil of a sparrow, wings spread. Her dark brown hair had been pulled back in a messy bun, her helm was under her arm, and snow was collecting on her hair. She smiled politely when she saw Ava and bowed.

"May I present Ethne Cawthorne, the Knight of the Sparrow," said Liadan.

Ava lifted her brows, impressed. "*The* Cawthornes?"

"The very ones. At your service, your highness," the apparent Ethne said, smiling.

The Cawthornes were an ancient and noble house and had turned out some of the best warriors in the seven kingdoms. Ava wasn't surprised that a Cawthorne was friends with the likes of Liadan: it would take a true warrior to keep up with the Knight of the Wild.

"She is my fiercest and most loyal friend," went on Liadan proudly, "and we have shed blood for each other. She can be trusted."

Ava nodded graciously at the knight. This Ethne, like Liadan, was tousled, breathless, and stained in blood. So Liadan hadn't stormed the castle corridors alone. She owed both knights a debt of gratitude.

"I am in your debt for keeping my Liadan safe," Ava said to the knight.

"I am in your debt for ensnaring her heart," returned Ethne with a crooked smile. "'Tis about time my dearest friend knew a woman's touch. Most of her life hath been a dry spell, if you can believe it, and she would scold those who would seek pleasure themselves—"

"Ethne!" Liadan growled, tensing up.

Ava giggled behind her hand. Then her eyes went to Lysa, who shrank beneath her gaze. She felt guilty to see Lysa so miserable and meek: while journeying through the passages, Liadan had told her how Lysa had been forced to betray her, and how it was Lysa who had come to Liadan, begging that she save Ava from her marriage.

"Do not cringe, dearest Lysa," said Ava soothingly. "All is forgiven. I did not understand before, but I understand your predicament now."

A look of relief passed through Lysa's brown eyes. She moved close, still a little meek but happy now. "Here," she said, pulling a gown from her bundle. "I managed to slip into your bedchamber and get you some clothes. I brought you a cloak as well . . ."

"And no one noticed you?" said Ava in surprise.

Lysa smiled. "No one notices peasants, your highness," she said, and for some reason, she caught eyes with Ethne and gave her a reproving look. Ethne only smiled as if she wanted to say something – perhaps some joke – but deciding better, the knight held her tongue. Ava stared at the two, wondering at their silent exchange.

"Here," Lysa said again, holding out the gown. It was pale blue, one of Ava's simple traveling gowns.

Remembering that she was naked beneath Liadan's cloak, Ava sighed in relief. "You are so sweet to me, Lysa," she said, and Lysa blushed. Ava dropped the cloak away, revealing her nudity, and saw the Knight of the Sparrow's intrigued eyes immediately go to her great breasts. Liadan's lips tightened, and seeing this, Ethne laughed, rolled her eyes, and looked away.

Holding back a laugh, Ava looked at Lysa, who was blushing bright as she avoided looking at Ava's body. "Help me dress!" Ava said, gesturing. "Quickly!"

Once Ava had donned her gown and fur cloak, Liadan put her own cloak back on again. "Lift me, my knight!" Ava regally commanded, and the Knight of the Wild obeyed, taking Ava by the waist and lifting her easily onto the dark brown horse – Ava's lashes fluttered in delight – before mounting behind her and taking the reins.

Ethne likewise attempted to lift Lysa by the waist, but Lysa was having none of it. She smacked Ethne's reaching gauntlets away, and with a haughty jerk of her chin, clumsily mounted the horse herself with the bundle clutched haphazardly under one arm.

Ava knew Lysa had never ridden a horse in her life and would have been better off allowing Ethne to help her. Everyone watched the handmaiden scramble, and by the time she had straightened up, her brown hair was in her face. She impatiently smacked it back and avoided everyone's eye.

Ethne, meanwhile, seemed very amused by Lysa's clear disdain for her. Smirking, she climbed up into the saddle behind Lysa and reached around her, taking the reins. One of her strong arms closed sudden and hard around Lysa to keep her from falling sideways when she suddenly slipped, and Ava saw Lysa blush with an odd mixture of pleasure and embarrassment. The little handmaiden didn't meet anyone's eye as the knights snapped their reins and the horses took off.

Despite everything that was happening, Ava couldn't help feeling joyously unchained. She was finally, finally free of her marriage, her duty, and a life she had never wanted, finally free to live as she pleased, do as she pleased! She loved the feel of Liadan's hard armor brushing her back, the heat of Liadan's breath on her ear, the way the racing horse made her heart thunder in her chest as they bounced along.

Glancing over, Ava noticed how Lysa's small breasts were bouncing behind her gown. Her cloak had blown open as the white stallion carried her and Ethne forward, and Ethne could be seen occasionally peering over Lysa's shoulder at her jiggling breasts. What was more, Lysa seemed to know this was happening and enjoyed taunting the knight. She was deliberately allowing her cloak to hang open and had allowed her laces to sag a little loose as well.

As they were racing along, Ava managed to catch Lysa's eye. Lysa's brown eyes sparkled mischievously, and they grinned at each other.

They rode for a day and a night, putting as much distance between themselves and Castle Caradin as possible. It wasn't until they stopped in a little wood to camp that it occurred to Ava to even wonder where they were going. She was exhausted and sore from the ride, she was hungry, she was cold. What would they do for food? She didn't know how to hunt. She didn't know how to do . . . anything, and the realization was both embarrassing and painful. She couldn't even sew her own clothes, a skill most princesses learned at a fairly young age.

Ava felt useless as everyone else set about building the camp. Ethne went off to gather firewood (Ava offered to help but was told it was too dangerous), and when that was done, Liadan cast golden light from her hands, creating a fire that spread its delicious warmth over the camp. Lysa then took out a few hares she'd stolen from Caradin's kitchen and started preparing a stew with her little cauldron. So everyone else contributed . . . while Ava sat there and was waited on. She hated it. So to compensate, Ava ordered everyone around and pretended she had assigned them their tasks.

No one was cruel to Ava about her seeming ineptitude and haughtiness. Instead, they all seemed quite amused and pretended as if they hadn't noticed.

And so, as the sun rose over the gray wintry sky, they ate hare stew and bread and discussed their plans for the journey ahead.

"So we are headed to a temple in Hastow?" asked Ava, confused. "But why?"

"Sanctuary," said Liadan, gazing grimly into the fire. "At first, Ethne and I were just going there for work. But now . . . Now the king of Almara will be after us. He'll want justice for his sons. A temple would offer sanctuary. We would be safe from the law there."

"But you said there was an assassin in the courtyard," said Lysa, just as confused as Ava, it seemed. "Wouldn't they believe the assassin responsible for the princes?"

Ethne shook her head. "Would be mighty convenient, wouldn't it? Except Ava is missing, and now, so is Liadan. Once King Eyvor realizes she's left the capital, he'll put two and two together—"

"And make six. Then I shall be blamed for Elric's sons," added Liadan darkly, "and in truth, I did slay one of them. I would deserve execution."

"Don't say that!" said Ava at once. "You were defending my honor! Prince Cristen got what he deserved." She glared into space, remembering how the prince had torn her gown and pulled her hair.

"Whatever the case," said Ethne, "we shall move on to Hastow and seek sanctuary, then we shall make our move from there."

"We could away to Wildoras," said Liadan thoughtfully. "My people wouldn't ask questions if I returned, so long as I didn't return to my own tribe. And all of you would be welcome there."

"Hmm. I suppose we have no other options," said Ethne tiredly. "We'll be wanted across the seven kingdoms now. There'll be a bounty on our heads and nowhere to run."

Ava stared at her feet. The initial euphoria of her sudden freedom had washed away, and now the cold, hard reality of exile was settling over her. She would never have a normal life, with a home and a warm bed. Not in the seven kingdoms, anyway. And unless they made it to Wildoras, they would always live on the run.

Ava looked up when she felt the back of Liadan's gentle fingers touching her cheek. The knight had removed her gauntlets to eat her stew, and her blue eyes as she gazed down at Ava were warm and kind.

"Fear not, my love," Liadan said in her pleasant, deep alto. "I shall protect you with my life, and we shall survive this together, you and I. I did not risk everything to take you from the castle only to perish now."

Ava gazed up at tall Liadan and managed a trembling smile, thinking how she loved her so much.

After supper, Ethne volunteered to take first watch as the others rested. The knights spread out their bedrolls, and Ava was amused to see Lysa realizing she would have to share a bedroll with Ethne when the time came. For now, however, she would sleep in Ethne's bedroll alone as the Knight of the Sparrow sat beside the fire, guarding the camp.

Ava cuddled up in Liadan's bedroll with her. The knight kept her armor on (the better to be ready for a fight) but left her gauntlets off to the side. She lay on her back, staring at the stars, as Ava lay on her back beside her, sinking in the massive nest of her golden hair. The sheepskin spread over them, stopping under their chins.

"I thought I would never see you again," Liadan whispered very low, so that Ethne would not hear from her seat at the fire. On the other side of Liadan, Lysa was sleeping peacefully in Ethne's bedroll.

"I thought the same," said Ava sadly, thinking on that horrible day and how everything had seemed to go so wrong: first Liadan was taken from her, then Prince Cassian was murdered, she was almost killed by an assassin and nearly assaulted by Prince Cristen, and then she was forced to flee with a bounty likely now on Liadan's head . . .

Hopefully, it would all be worth it in the end. Ava couldn't imagine she would have been happy had she stayed behind, even with both Cassian and Cristen dead. Her father would have just married her off to another prince to form another alliance. At least now she was free . . . for however long it lasted.

"I shall always be your knight," Liadan said earnestly. "Nothing and no one shall part us again."

Ava glanced over and her heart leapt in her throat: Liadan was gazing at her with that intense fire in her eyes. Ava felt the knight's hand reaching under the sheepskin, searching for her. The hand found one of her breasts and squeezed it firmly through the fabric, so that Ava blushed. She immediately felt the blood rush to her sex, the swell of arousal between her thighs, the pump of her eager clitoris, and Liadan smiled as if she could tell how much Ava desired her.

Put your hands on me, Ava thought, breathless with arousal. *Those hard, strong hands . . .* "Liadan," she whispered aloud, "make love to me . . ."

Liadan obeyed. The knight roughly unlaced the front of Ava's gown, until her heaving breasts rose from it, lifting and falling with her anxious breaths, and ducking her head under the sheepskin, Liadan buried her face in Ava's breast and suckled ravenously on her rigid pink nipple, so that Ava gasped. The hard, strong hand that Ava loved so much groped under her skirt and slid down her panties, and as Liadan roughly fingered Ava's sex and sucked hard at her nipple, Ava moaned and arched her back against the pleasure, thrusting out her big breasts and sighing in delight.

THEY CONTINUED ON DUE east, always pressing toward Hastow, and due largely to the snow, they had little choice but to keep to the open road and risk encountering other travelers. For this reason, they traveled always at night and camped near the woods during the day, as the roads were far busier during daylight.

Ava had never camped before, let alone left Caradin Castle. She found it difficult, if not downright agony, sleeping on the hard ground, in the cold, and eating dried meat and aging bread, wearing the same smelly gown every day. She missed her beautiful gowns and jewelry, missed her big soft bed and the fire in her bedchamber. She missed hot roasted meat and fresh bread warm from the oven....

But suffer as she did, spoiled princess though she was, Ava was determined not to complain or show discomfort. Especially not to Liadan, a barbarian warrior who had lived much of her childhood in the wild, in forests, hunting wild boar and sleeping on the ground. Their rough, cold days and nights were probably trivial to Liadan, and Ava did not want to appear spoiled or weak before her.

Ava also had to admit that she was terrified. If they were captured before they could claim sanctuary in Hastow, Liadan would be executed, and so would Lysa and Ethne for aiding her. Even if Ava's father would rather spare them, to do so would risk open war with Almara, who would want Liadan punished. King Eyvor's hand would be forced.

But as Ava lay awake with her anxious thoughts, Liadan remained as calm and resigned as usual. The way she carried on, it were as if they were back at the castle, Ava thought – as if Prince Cassian and the assassin had never happened. They would be lying in their bedroll together, and then Liadan would grab Ava, roughly undo her gown, and grope her and finger her to a sobbing climax – so casually, and yet with such confidence and strength that Ava shuddered as she grew moist.

Some mornings, when it was Liadan's turn to keep watch, Ava would sit up with her. She would sit on the knight's lap, and Liadan would stroke her hair, and as the others slept nearby in their bedroll, they would speak in whispers of their lives.

Because of Liadan, Ava was now so fascinated with the barbarians of Wildoras that she felt like her father. But she couldn't help it. She wanted to know everything about Liadan – not just about her culture but also her personal life: her family, her friends, what it was like to live at the knight academy in the capital. Everything.

Serious, dutiful Liadan was always patient, if not amused by Ava's questions, and answered readily, one gauntlet absently stroking Ava's long golden tresses as the princess sat in her lap.

"No, Ethne was not my only friend, thank the gods," Liadan said in answer to Ava's question. She sounded quite amused.

It was another white wintry morning, and they were camping on the edge of the wood, as birds chirped, and streams of cold sunlight fell over the snowbanks. Liadan had lit a fire yet again with her magick, and its golden light spilled hot over them. The flames were like liquid, twisting and rising from the circle of stone.

"No, I was not ostracized. Though I am a foreigner, there is much respect for my people in your land," Liadan went on. "I was welcomed warmly when I did arrive and had many friends. Ethne was simply the closest. Perhaps because we were both exiles and bonded over the fact. She and I, though different in temperament, are alike in many ways."

Ava's brows went up in surprise, and she looked over to the bedroll where Ethne slept on her back beside Lysa. "Ethne was exiled?" she cried in amazement. "For what?"

Liadan hesitated. "It is not my place to tell you, sweet princess. Ethne is deeply ashamed of what transpired. Perhaps she shall tell you herself one day, if you gently inquire."

Ava didn't quite know what to think. The Cawthornes were upstanding people not given to crime or cruelty. That one of their own had been exiled meant the crime a grave matter. Had Ethne killed someone? Ava found it hard to imagine smiling, joking Ethne a murderer, though she had to admit she had noticed a foul temper in the otherwise gentle knight: while they were resting on the side of the road, Ethne had viciously kicked a tree over some trivial matter, shocking Lysa.

Liadan, meanwhile, was the exact opposite. The Knight of the Wild was cold in her anger. She had cut off Prince Cristen's head quite dispassionately and had only shown emotion when worried for Ava.

"What of your other friends at the academy?" Ava asked.

"There were twenty other women in our year," Liadan answered, "and seventy-men, all brave and righteous and loyal allies. Two were good friends with Ethne and I. There was Saoirse, the Knight of the Lion. She hailed from City Arina not far from here. A very loyal friend and a mighty warrior. She wasn't exactly in our year, but she was well-respected in the academy, and we took to her."

"What was she like?" Ava asked curiously.

Liadan smiled. "Golden hair like yours, though quite thick and wild. She was always very serious and not given much to speech. A proper warrior."

Ava held back a laugh: Liadan approved of Saoirse because she was so like herself. "And the other one?" she asked.

"The other was known as Rowan, the Knight of Thorns, a sigil she made herself."

"What did she look like?"

"A dark-haired warrior. She was a princess once, like you."

Ava looked up at Liadan, startled. "Truly?"

"Aye," answered Liadan. "She was princess of Realm Almara and sister of Prince Cassian and Prince Cristen."

Ava stared. "It can't be true. I have never heard of the princes having a sister!"

"And nor would you," answered Liadan darkly. "Rowan was stricken from the records and exiled to the academy at quite a young age."

Ava's mouth fell open. "But why?"

"When she was a child, she was seen kissing another girl. Her father was ashamed and sent her away to hide the disgrace. They do not tolerate women like us in Almara."

Ava stared at her lap, realizing for the first time just how much her father had cared for her. King Eyvor had known since Ava was a child that she fancied women. It was half the reason he had chosen Lysa to be her companion: Lysa was rumored to fancy other girls as a child and had been shamed for it publicly in the market. The king hadn't wanted his daughter to live alone or to believe there was no one in the world like her.

Perhaps King Eyvor had thought Ava only fancied feminine women and that she could never love or desire a big, masculine barbarian like Liadan. And yet, Ava had spent years longing in secret for the women knights at Caradin. What a fool her father had been.

Ava realized she must have looked unhappy, for she felt Liadan's gauntlet soothingly stroking her hair again.

"Won't Rowan be angry you slew her brother?" Ava asked to change the subject.

To Ava's surprise, Liadan chuckled. "On the contrary, your highness," said the knight, amused, "she would shower me with kisses. She was always very playful in that regard."

"Did she not love her brother?" cried Ava, shocked.

"Cristen used to bully her to tears," Liadan answered darkly, "so no. She did not."

Ava used to long for siblings when she was a child. Now she wondered if her lonely childhood hadn't been something of a blessing. Besides, she hadn't been *that* lonely, for she'd had Lysa.

"And your sister?" Ava asked. "Didn't she attend the same academy?"

"No," answered Liadan a little sadly. "She was sent to another academy in Realm Truever but sought work in Hastow to be nearer to me." Liadan smiled, gazing off happily. "Ceana is a sweet creature and good to the bone. You will love her." She looked down at Ava. "And she shall love you like family."

Ava smiled to see the affection in Liadan's eyes. "I wish I could meet all your family," she said. "What would it be like if we lived with your tribe? I know we could not, but still, I wonder."

Liadan gazed off wistfully. "Had I been my mother's eldest daughter, I would have been queen." She looked down at Ava and affectionately pinched her chin. "You would be my woman, and I would love and protect you, as I do now, only there would be no constant fear of capture and execution, and we would have many strong daughters."

Ava laughed, delighted. "But how? We're two women!"

Liadan only smiled. "Wildoras women are beings of magick. We have the blood of the first people, from a time when there were no men. There are ways." She released Ava's chin, looked past her, and said no more.

NOW THAT THE THOUGHT of living in Wildoras had been put in Ava's mind, it was difficult to stop daydreaming. She was a princess. She had always expected to enter an arranged marriage, have sex she didn't want or enjoy, and have unwanted children with a man she felt nothing for.

Now, for the first time in her life, a happy marriage was a possibility. She was bubbling inside with joy. For even though Liadan could not return to her tribe and could not become queen, there was still the possibility of a carefree life in the wild. Wildoras was outside of the law of the seven realms: none of the kingdoms would dare march on a nation of magi warriors just to avenge Prince Cassian and Prince Cristen.

Because she couldn't contain her excitement, Ava found herself giggling about her daydreams with Lysa one morning as they gathered firewood. They had started on the edge of the wood, as Ethne was worried about them going too far into the trees, and the knights were not thirty feet away at the camp, where they were setting up stones for the fire and tending the horses. But Ava, foolish and rebellious, had led them deeper into the trees, the better to find more firewood.

"So the legends are true," said Lysa in wonder, her thin arms full of sticks. "The women of Wildoras *can* reproduce woman with woman! I had always thought those fairytales, but I can't see why Liadan would lie to you. I wonder how it's done."

"Liadan said her people have ancient blood from a time when there were no men," Ava said thoughtfully. "I thought perchance it were some spell, but now I am thinking it were baser than that."

"I didn't know you wanted children," said Lysa curiously.

Ava bent down, collected another stick, and added it to the bundle in her arms, her golden hair swinging back as she stood again. "Well, that was before, when I thought I must marry a man. Now that I know I can have children with Liadan, I can think of little else. They would be beautiful and wild, some with red hair, some with gold." She smiled dreamily.

Lysa smiled. "You are really quite taken with her. It is sweet."

Ava angled her pale lashes down and blushed prettily. But it was true. She felt overwhelmed by her love for her Liadan, and she was excited to spend many happy years with her.

"And you are taken with Ethne," Ava teased, "though you shant admit it." She laughed when Lysa blushed indignantly.

"I am not taken with that *dog*!" Lysa hotly declared.

Ava stopped laughing and gently implored, "But why do you hate her so?"

"She's arrogant," Lysa said at once. "She thinks I am beneath her! A piece of meat! A conquest for her to brag about to Liadan! I am nothing to her—" Lysa's words halted in her throat when an arrow zipped by her head, missing her by inches.

Ava screamed as another arrow came and grabbed Lysa, pulling her to the ground. They fell in the snow in a spray of white, dropping their bundles of firewood.

Ava sat up on her elbow and pushed the hair back from her face in time to see men in ragged leathers – bandits!—approaching through the trees. There were three of them, unshaven and rank, with stringy hair. One bandit had a bow and the other two were carrying chipped swords. The one with the bow lowered his weapon so his friends could approach ahead of him.

"What do we have here?" said the tallest man, sword in hand. "Two little rabbits lost in the woods! And such fat tits!" He looked at Lysa with greedy eyes, and the handmaiden shrank down in terror. "Gonna take my time with these ones!"

The other bandits laughed.

Lysa grabbed Ava's arm and cringed against her. Tears were already streaming down her face. Ava went to hold her and soothe her, but the tall bandit grabbed Lysa by the hair and dragged her to him, screaming. He yanked Lysa to her feet, grinning all the while, and as his friends laughed, he tugged at Lysa's dress, so that one of her breasts shivered free.

"Leave her alone!" Ava screamed angrily, heart racing.

Lysa twisted and fought to get away, but the bandit held on, chuckling darkly. He groped her breast in a hard hand, and blushing angrily, Lysa screamed and elbowed him in the face in a spurt of blood. The bandit cursed ("Foul wench!") and released Lysa, clutching his bloody mouth and nose. Lysa fell on hands and knees in the snow, panting shrilly.

"Ethne!" Lysa screamed, tears in her eyes. "ETHNE!"

"Shut her up!" snarled the tall bandit, and to Ava's horror, the bandit with the bow nocked an arrow and grinned as he aimed it at the back of Lysa's head. But he didn't have a chance to shoot – a stream of golden fire hit him full in the face, and he fell down in the snow, screaming and flailing, until he suddenly fell still. He was dead.

The other two bandits barely had time to look around: the second bandit choked as Liadan thrust her sword – which was glowing with golden fire – straight through his belly. He coughed golden fire and blood, his eyes distant in shock, and when Liadan viciously ripped the blazing sword free, he fell down dead.

Meanwhile, the tall bandit who had assaulted Lysa was cut off mid-scream as Ethne's sword flashed around and took off his head. As his shocked head bounced away, trailing blood across the blank snow, his body remained standing a moment, blood squirting from the neck, before suddenly collapsing.

"My princess," said Liadan, her voice trembling, "did they hurt you?" She knelt before Ava, and her frightened blue eyes searched Ava's face.

It took Ava a moment to realize she was crying – not for herself but for Lysa. With a sob, she fell forward in Liadan's arms and closed her eyes for a moment, relieved and soothed to feel the strength of the knight's hard embrace.

Ava opened her eyes again when she heard singing: Ethne was kneeling and holding Lysa in her arms. Lysa was clinging to her and sobbing desperately. Ethne kissed Lysa's brown hair, stroked her hair down, and sang in a low, soft voice. Her voice was surprisingly pretty, and Lysa, wrapped in the knight's strong embrace, happily closed her eyes and relaxed as Ethne's sweet song carried for her.

The Knight of the Sparrow indeed.

Don't miss out!

Visit the website below and you can sign up to receive emails whenever Ash Gray publishes a new book. There's no charge and no obligation.

https://books2read.com/r/B-A-ZRKF-XNDBC

BOOKS 2 READ

Connecting independent readers to independent writers.

Also by Ash Gray

A Time of Darkness
Time's Arrow
The Infinite Athenaeum

Clan of the Cave Bear
Taken by the Chieftess
Passed Around
Keeping Warm
Her Pretty Pet
Dominated
Seduced
Caught
Savaged

Cyber Mech
Good With Her Hands

Fallen Stars

Handfasting the Warrior Queen
The Revenge of Raven's Cross
The Light of Lythara
Taming the Wolf Knight
The Mermaids of Menosea
The Fairy Queen of Elwenhal
The Dragon of Edhen
Essential Selene
Hearth and Home
Aereth's Return
The Fairy Ring
The Main Course
Knights of Passion: The Complete Series

Knights of Vallor
Saving Salia
Raven Spirit
Eryet's Fountain
The Daughter of Idet
The Mirror of Iovar
Aine's Athenaeum
Bone and Fire
Princess Eydis

Ona of Ozmora
The Amulet of Tizra
The Bandit Queen of Crystal Falls
The Council of Eldor
The Sword of Avara
Wicked Things in the Wilds

The Dragon Riders of Valheera
Birthday Surprises

The Dreamscape
Out of Mind
Recalling Color

The Last Queen of Qorlec
Project Mothership
The Harvest
The Suns of Anarchy
The Light-year Lion
Moon Fire
Exiled Stars
Zora's Stone

The Legend of Kiva
The Starlight Stair

The Pussycat Chronicles
The Heist
Broken Hearts and Brain Damage
Candy, Sweat, and Regret
Lip Gloss and Loose Women

Witch Xim
Rezzora's Workshop

Standalone
Qorth
Fall Apart World
Unicorn Blood

About the Author

Ash Gray is a lesbian living in California. She writes lesfic (aka fiction for lesbians) in science fiction, fantasy, and paranormal settings.